WRITTEN AND ILLUSTRATED BY
SAXTON FREYMANN

Gus *and* Button

ARTHUR A. LEVINE BOOKS
AN IMPRINT OF SCHOLASTIC PRESS
NEW YORK

Waiting at the window for the whirling storm to stop,
Gus saw something green blow by and watched it gently drop.

Dashing out, he picked it up and quickly turned around
to face the Howling Forest that surrounded his whole town.

Gus knew it was a dangerous place where he must never go.
"But I must find out," said Gus, "where things this bright can grow.
I'll discover all the things that I have never seen!
I'm sure that I will find them, for my eyes are very keen."

Deep within the forest,
something *KNOCKED* Gus to the ground.
"What kind of tree are *YOU?*" said Gus.
"Did someone chop you down?
I hope you're feeling better soon.
I'm Gus, it's nice to meet you."
The big wolf laughed. "My name is Howell.
I WAS about to eat you.
But you're too *SILLY!*" grinned the wolf,
and vanished in the night.
"That tree's BARK," Gus giggled,
"is much worse than its *BITE!*"

They wandered on, for miles and miles, until the break of day,
calling as the sun came up, "*HELP!* We've lost our way!"
"We'll save you!" came some voices. "…Just a moment please!"
The travelers stopped and stared at what was coming through the trees.

"Hello, I'm Belle," the pepper said, "and who on earth are you?"
"Explorers," Gus said proudly, "and we crossed the Forest, too!"
"You crossed the wolfy woods?" gasped Belle. "That is just incredible!
Either you are very brave, or you must be inedible."

Cecil led them through some trees and to a mossy field,
and out across the water, *Cornucopia* was revealed.
Button gave a bark and wagged his tail from side to side.
Gus bounded down the bushy bank to where the boat was tied.

"All aboard!" The merry crew set out across the bay.
Gus's crazy dancing rocked the boat along the way.
"Gus!" warned Pip. "Be careful, or you'll fall out of the boat!"
Gus balanced on the bow and laughed, "Don't worry! I can float!"

"Slow down, my friend," said Belle, as Gus spun 'round excitedly.
"The more you look at something, the more that you will see."
Gus pointed to a pumpkin and he asked, "Who lives in there?"
Cecil giggled, Pip turned red, and Belle said, "That's our Mayor."

They climbed a hill above the bay and Gus began to dance.
He shrugged when Cecil warned him to look out for wild ants.
Belle said, "I'm afraid that he'll discover very soon
that THAT'S an ANT up in that tree and not a red balloon!"

Far from giant pumpkins, far from wild ants,
they wandered in a garden of exotic flowering plants.
Gus heard a sobbing sound and Belle leaned closer to his ear,
"Ms. Green is brokenhearted since her baby disappeared.
A sudden storm, a whirling wind, blew Benny off the ground.
We've searched and searched for Benny Green, but he has not been found."

A light went on in Gus's head. He pointed to his pack.
He galloped through the garden. "Look, Ms. Green! I've brought him back!"
"Benny! Welcome *HOME* again," cheered everyone with glee.
Gus blushed and whispered, "Button, was there *MORE* I didn't see?"

Pip said, "Gus and Button, I think you should get home too.
And to see you get home safely, I think we should go with you."
They traveled, laughing, singing songs. They were not afraid.
Gus felt safe and happy with the friends that he had made.

Surrounded by a happy crowd, Gus said, "Listen well.
These very special friends of mine are Cecil, Pip, and Belle.
They showed me many lovely things and helped me realize
that to really see what's out there, you need more than open eyes.
When I keep my wits about me and I keep an open mind,
EVERYWHERE I look I am surprised by what I find!"

Then Benny and Ms. Green dropped in, to everyone's surprise,
to shower them with flowers from the rosy evening skies.
That was something no one in the town had ever seen,
and nothing in that town's the same, since Gus saved Benny Green.

ALL OF THE PICTURES IN THIS BOOK WERE COMPOSED ENTIRELY OF FOOD.

Because of the complexity of the images and the speed with which sliced fruits and vegetables discolor, each object was carved and photographed separately. These photographs were then scanned and collaged together on the computer. None of the characters or objects were created, enhanced, or altered on the computer. The one exception to this is that occasional liberties were taken with scale: Portobello mushroom tops were enlarged to serve as the ground in the mushroom town, and some vegetables were made slightly bigger to serve as buildings. Every effort was made to keep the ingredients as pure as possible.

HERE ARE SOME OF THE FOODS TO LOOK FOR IN THE BOOK: *(in order of appearance)*

Mushrooms, black-eyed peas, peas, artichokes, bell peppers, apples, oranges, lentils, broccoli, broccolini, broccoflower, parsley, red cabbages, watermelons, bananas, apricots, pears, sweet potatoes, fingerling potatoes, chives, poppyseeds, grapefruits, turnips, carrots, radishes, starfruits, peaches, habanero peppers, butternut squash, leeks, dates, tomatoes, figs, carnival squash, acorn squash, honeydew melon, pomegranates, onions, celery, canary melons, prickly pears, daikon radishes, cucumbers, lemons, eggplants, Japanese eggplants, avocados, okra, pumpkins, pickles, cherries, thyme, Swiss chard, pineapples, blueberries, kumquats, patty pan squash, lychees, beets, red kori squash.

Library of Congress Cataloging-in-Publication Data

Freymann, Saxton.
Gus and Button / by Saxton Freymann and Joost Elffers.
p. cm.
Summary: Gus and his dog Button leave their white world to brave the scary forest and discover color.
ISBN 0-439-11015-7
[1. Color—Fiction 2. Dogs—Fiction. 3. Stories in rhyme.] I. Elffers, Joost. II. Title.

PZ8.3.F91123 Gu 2001
[E]—dc21   00-062075

Book design by Erik Thé
Photography by Nimkin/Parrinello

10 9 8 7 6 5 4 3 2 1   01 02 03 04 05

Printed in Mexico   49
First edition, October 2001

For Mom and Pop, who let me cross the forest.
S.F.